D0337092

THIS BLOOMSBURY BOOK

BELONGS TO

....

To my mum and dad,
and James

This edition published for Igloo Books Ltd in 2007

First published in Great Britain in 1999 by Bloomsbury Publishing Plc
38 Soho Square, London W1V 5DF

Text and illustrations copyright © Joy Gosney 1999
The moral right of the author has been asserted.

All rights reserved.
No part of this publication may be reproduced
or transmitted by any means, electronic, mechanical, photocopying
or otherwise without the prior permission of the publisher.

A CIP catalogue record for this book is available from the British Library.
ISBN 0 7475 4740 8 (paperback)
ISBN 0 7475 4475 1 (hardback)

Designed by Dawn Apperley

Printed and bound in China by South China Printing Co.

3 5 7 9 10 8 6 4 2

Naughty Parents

Joy Gosney

I love my mum and dad but they do like getting into mischief.

So one day, when they said we were going to the park to see the ducks, I decided to keep a sharp eye on them.

But as soon as we reached
the duck pond, Mum and Dad
were **very** naughty!

They went down the wrong path
together ... and got lost!

"I can't find my parents anywhere!"
I told the ducks.
"What shall I do?"

"We saw them running to the playground," they said. "You might find them there."

My naughty parents were being naughty.
"**Oh no!**" gasped a lady.
"They'll land in the dirt!"

When I arrived in the playground,
I saw a nice lady.
"Have you seen my naughty parents?"
I asked.
"Yes, I saw them sliding down the
slide and getting dirty!" said the lady.
But I couldn't see them anywhere.

They had already run off ...

... to find some puddles. My naughty parents were being **very** naughty now!

"Oh stop!" shouted a man. "I'm soaked!"

I hurried on, until I found a grumpy man. "Have you seen my naughty parents?" I asked.

"Oh yes! I saw them jumping in puddles and they made me all wet!" said the man.
But I couldn't see them anywhere.

They had already run off ...

... to buy ice-creams.
My naughty parents had
never been **SO** naughty!

"Oh dear!" giggled a woman.
"Your ice-creams are melting!"

I hurried after my naughty parents,
until I saw a kind woman.
"Have you seen my naughty parents?"
I asked.
"I have, and they were eating sticky
ice-cream!" said the woman.
But I still couldn't see them anywhere.

They had already run off.

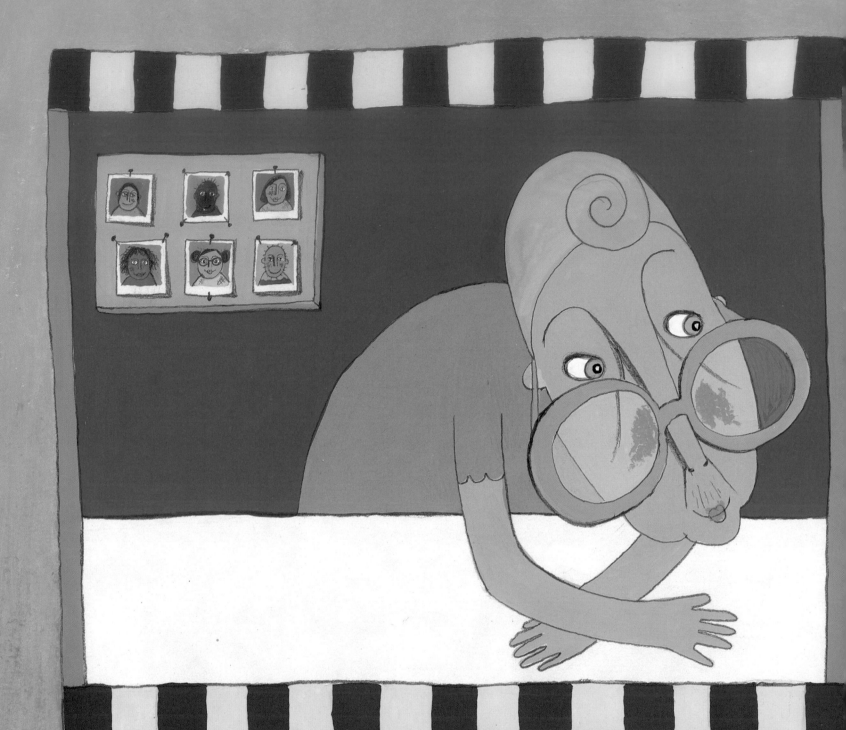

By now I was getting worried, so I went straight to the missing parents booth and told the lady everything that had happened.

"Ah yes!" said the lady. "I have two **very dirty, wet** and **sticky** parents here, who fit that description. They must belong to you!"

At last, I had found them!
Since that day, Mum and Dad have

been very good ...

I wonder why?